A NOTE TO PARENTS

Reading Aloud with Your Child

Research shows that reading books aloud is the single most valuable support parents can provide in helping children learn to read.

- Be a ham! The more enthusiasm you display, the more your child will enjoy the book.
- Run your finger underneath the words as you read to signal that the print carries the story.
- Leave time for examining the illustrations more closely; encourage your child to find things in the pictures.
- Invite your youngster to join in whenever there's a repeated phrase in the text.
- Link up events in the book with similar events in your child's life.
- If your child asks a question, stop and answer it. The book can be a means to learning more about your child's thoughts.

Listening to Your Child Read Aloud

The support of your attention and praise is absolutely crucial to your child's continuing efforts to learn to read.

- If your child is learning to read and asks for a word, give it immediately so that the meaning of the story is not interrupted. DO NOT ask your child to sound out the word.
- On the other hand, if your child initiates the act of sounding out, don't intervene.
- If your child is reading along and makes what is called a miscue, listen for the sense of the miscue. If the word "road" is substituted for the word "street," for instance, no meaning is lost. Don't stop the reading for a correction.
- If the miscue makes no sense (for example, "horse" for "house"), ask your child to reread the sentence because you're not sure you understand what's just been read.
- Above all else, enjoy your child's growing command of print and make sure you give lots of praise. *You are your child's first teacher—and the most important one. Praise from you is critical for further risk-taking and learning.*

—Priscilla Lynch
Ph.D., New York University
Educational Consultant

ONGS TO:

ANK

ISBN 0-590-98481-0

SJSC21

12 11 10 9 8 7 6 5 4 3 2 1   6 7 8 9/9 0 1/0

Designed by Joan Ferrigno

Printed in the U.S.A.   23

First Scholastic printing, November 1996

Adapted by Kimberly Weinberger
From the screenplay written by
Leo Benvenuti & Steve Rudnick and Timothy Harris & Herschel Weingrod

Hello Reader! — Level 3

SCHOLASTIC INC.

New York Toronto London Auckland Sydney

CHAPTER 1

It was a slow day at the space park.
Swackhammer, the big boss of the
park, was not happy.
He was not very nice, either.
"We need something new!"
Swackhammer shouted.
"Something that will make people
want to come here."
"Yes, something new!" answered his
tiny alien workers, the Nerdlucks.
"What we need," said Swackhammer
slowly, "is something *looney*.
Go to Earth and get the Looney
Tunes. Bring them here to me!"

And so
the Nerdlucks
were on their way.
They flew toward Earth and
landed in Looney Tune Land.
The Nerdlucks stepped off their ship.
They came face-to-face with
Bugs Bunny.
"What's up, Doc?" asked Bugs.

"Hold on there, Mr. Looney Tune,"
said Pound, the leader
of the Nerdlucks.
"Get the bunny! Get the bunny!"
said the other aliens.
They pointed their space
guns at Bugs.
They had caught their first
Looney Tune!

The news about Bugs Bunny
spread fast.
The Looney Tunes called
an important meeting with
the Nerdlucks.
At the meeting, the Nerdlucks told
of their plan to bring the Looney
Tunes back to their space park.
When the aliens finished speaking,
they began to board their ship.
"Not so fast, Doc," said Bugs Bunny.
"You have to give us a chance to
save ourselves."
The Nerdlucks agreed.

Then Bugs Bunny met with the other Looney Tunes.

"How can we beat those aliens?" asked Bugs.

"Well," said Daffy Duck, "they have small arms and short legs."

"And they're not very fast," added Elmer Fudd.

"They sure are tiny," said Sylvester.

"They can't jump high, either," said Porky Pig.

"Hmmmm," the Looney Tunes said together.

"We'll challenge them to a basketball game!" said Bugs Bunny. And that's exactly what they did.

CHAPTER 2

The Nerdlucks didn't know
anything about basketball.
But they did have a plan.
They went to a basketball game.
Many great players were there
that night.
During the game, Pound released
some *ooze* which turned into
purple air.
It flew into a player's ear.
The player began to make strange
noises.
He shook all over!

Then the purple air flew back out.
It became ooze again.
Pound put it in a bottle.
The player seemed fine.
But there was one important change.
He had no talent!
Pound had taken all of his
talent away.
Later, the little Nerdlucks took the
talent from four other great players.
They were sure they could not
be beaten!

The Looney Tunes were practicing
when the Nerdlucks walked into
the gym.
The aliens quickly swallowed the
talent from the bottle.
Suddenly, they all began to grow . . .
and grow . . . and GROW!
"Uh-oh!" said Bugs and Daffy
together.
"They're superstars!" said Daffy.
"They're monsters!" shouted Porky
Pig.
"No! They're *Monstars*!" cried
Sylvester.
"See you at the game," the new
Monstars laughed.
Bugs Bunny watched them leave.
"This calls for a small change in
plan," he said.

There was only one person who could help the Looney Tunes. They needed the player who was known around the world for his talent.

They needed Michael Jordan —
the greatest basketball player
of all time!

At that moment, Michael was playing
golf with his friends, Stan and Larry.
Bugs quickly thought of a plan.
The Tunes waited under the ground
of the golf course.
Michael hit his golf ball into a hole.
When he reached into the hole to get
the ball, Michael felt himself being
pulled underground.
Stan and Larry looked over at the
hole.
Michael was gone!

When he landed, Michael found
himself in Looney Tune Land.
He could hardly believe his eyes.
Bugs Bunny quickly told him their
problem.
"What I'm trying to say," said Bugs,
"is WE NEED YOUR HELP!"
"But I'm a baseball player, now,"
said Michael.
It was true.
Michael had stopped playing
basketball.
He was following his dream.
He wanted to be a baseball player.
But the Looney Tunes were sure that
Michael could save their team.

Just then, the Monstars crashed
through the wall.
When they heard that Michael
didn't want to play in the game,
they began to tease him.
"Maybe you're chicken!"
the aliens shouted.
Pound used his strong hands to crush
Michael into the shape of a ball.

"Look at your hero now!" said Pound.
He and the other Monstars passed
Michael back and forth.
Then Michael returned to his normal
shape.
When Tweety tried to defend Michael,
the Monstars slapped Tweety across
the room.
This made Michael very angry.
"Let's play some basketball," he said.

Bugs and Daffy went to Michael's
house to get his basketball clothes.
But they didn't know that they
were being watched.
Michael's friend, Stan, had
been looking for him since he
disappeared at the golf course.
Stan followed Bugs and Daffy
back to Looney Tune Land.

CHAPTER 3

It was time for the big game to begin.
Swackhammer had come all the way
from his space park to watch.
His Monstars were ready.
The Tune Squad — Michael and
the Looney Tunes — tried hard.
But they could not beat the
Monstars.
By the middle of the game,
the Tune Squad was losing by
almost 50 points.

During halftime, Stan hid himself in
the Monstars' locker room.
There, he heard the Monstars tell
how they had gotten their talent.
Stan ran to tell Michael what he
had heard.

The Tune Squad was ready
to give up.
"Wait!" shouted Bugs. "Michael,
you forgot your secret stuff."
The Looney Tunes each took a
drink from a bottle that read
"Michael's Secret Stuff."
Suddenly, they felt strong.
They were ready to beat anyone!

What they didn't know was that the
"secret stuff" was only water.
Bugs had written the label himself!
But it didn't matter.
They *thought* it made them strong ...
and so it did!
They believed in
themselves.

The game continued.
The Tune Squad raced
up and down the court.
Michael scored again and again.
In no time, the Monstars were
winning by only three points.

"Time out!" Swackhammer shouted,
pointing at Michael.
"Why didn't you get *him?*"
"He plays *baseball,* not basketball,"
the Monstars answered.
Swackhammer decided he wanted
Michael to come to his space park.
A new deal was made.
If the Tune Squad won,
Swackhammer would let them
stay in Looney Tune Land.
And, he would give back all of the
talent the aliens had taken.
But if the Monstars won, Michael
would go back to the park with the
aliens and work there forever.

Now the Monstars played harder
than ever.
Stan had to play for a Looney Tune
who had been hurt.
As the Monstars jumped on him,
Stan threw the ball.
It landed in the basket — *SWISH!*
Just two more points and the
Tune Squad would win!
Michael watched as Stan was
helped off the court.
Stan's whole body was flat,
like a pancake.
But in the *cartoon world,* he was able
to pop back to his normal shape.
This gave Michael an idea.

There were only ten seconds left
in the game.
Michael ran with the ball.
He jumped high into the air.
The Monstars tried to hold him
down.
But Michael used cartoon power.
He stretched his whole body.
He put the ball into the basket
just as the buzzer sounded.
The Tune Squad
had won the game!

CHAPTER 4

"Get the Looney Tunes!"
Swackhammer shouted at his
Monstars.
"Put them on the ship.
They're coming with us."
"No, we had a deal," said Michael.
"I lied," growled Swackhammer.
Michael turned to the Monstars.
"Why do you let him tell you
what to do?" he asked.
"Because he's bigger than we are,"
the Monstars said.
Then they thought for a minute.
"No, wait," they said. "He's
bigger than we *used* to be."

The Monstars sent Swackhammer
back into space.
They stayed behind.
They wanted to join the Looney
Tunes!

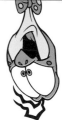

Michael had one more thing to do.
He took all of the talent back from
the Monstars.
He stored the talent in a basketball.
The Monstars became tiny
Nerdlucks again.

Then, Michael and Stan said
good-bye to the Looney Tunes
and went back to their world.

Michael found the five players
who had lost their talent.
As they all touched the basketball
at once, their talent came back.
Then Michael decided to return
to his old basketball team.
Thanks to the Looney Tunes,
he had found his love for
the game all over again.

The end. (That's all, folks!)